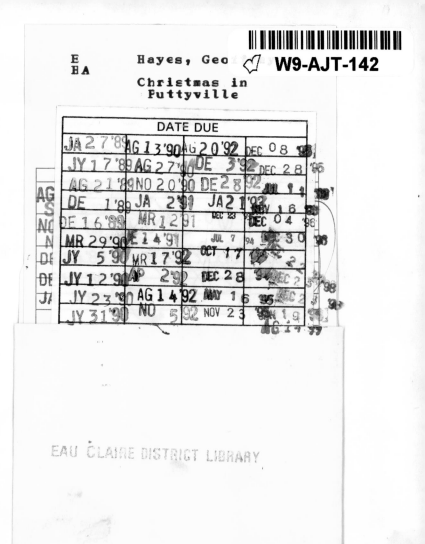

CHRISTMAS IN PUTTYVILLE

Geoffrey Hayes

Random House 🏠 New York

Copyright © 1985 by Geoffrey Hayes. All rights reserved under International and Pan-American Copyright Conventions. Published in the United States by Random House, Inc., New York, and simultaneously in Canada by Random House of Canada Limited, Toronto.

Library of Congress Cataloging in Publication Data: Hayes, Geoffrey. Christmas in Puttyville. SUMMARY: Weaver Bear and Little Sunshine want to make money to buy a Christmas tree, but their sympathy for a poor family changes their course of action. 1. Children's stories, American. [1. Christmas—Fiction. 2. Bears—Fiction] I. Title. PZ7.H31455Ch 1985 [Fic] 85-2009 ISBN: 0-394-87286-X (trade); 0-394-97286-4 (lib. bdg.) Manufactured in the United States of America 1 2 3 4 5 6 7 8 9 0

It was the day before Christmas. Weaver Bear and Little Sunshine were on their way to the Puttyville Fair to sell Christmas ornaments— painted pine cones, tinfoil stars, and buttons strung on yarn—that they had made themselves.

They were going to use the money to buy a tree for their clubhouse.

Most of the trees at Old Wolfgang's Christmas tree lot were too big. But the little one in the corner was just right.

Little Sunshine read the price tag. "Three dollars!" she gasped. "We'll have to sell a lot of ornaments to buy that!"

"May I help you?" asked Old Wolfgang.

"We're just looking for now," said Little Sunshine.

She and Weaver headed down the street.

The next person they saw was Ollie Arwood,
driving his wagon and singing:

GOOD FOOD

EAT SOME!
I MAKE IT
MYSELF!

"BUNS FOR YOUR BREAKFAST,
CAKES FOR YOUR TEA,
GINGERBREAD FOR CHRISTMAS,
BUY 'EM ALL FROM ME!"

"Hi, Mr. Arwood," said Weaver Bear.
"Do you want to buy some nice
Christmas ornaments?"

"I can't buy any because I haven't made any money yet today," said Ollie. "But how about a trade? I'll give you two gingerbread bears for one of those nice pine cones."

"We can hang the gingerbread bears on our tree before we eat them," said Sunshine.

"It's a deal!" said Weaver.

Ollie tied the pine cone to Crazy Horse's collar. Weaver Bear and Little Sunshine wished them both a Merry Christmas.

"We'd better get started," Little Sunshine told Weaver. "We haven't sold anything today either."

Weaver and Little Sunshine
walked down Main Street. It was
very crowded, and everyone was
too big or in too much of a
hurry to notice them.

Gifts

Galore

"Christmas tree stuff! Only ten cents apiece!" they shouted as loud as they could.

"Stop making so much racket!" complained Helga Barns. "I can't hear myself think!"

They moved a few feet away from Helga.
"Christmas tree stuff!" they cried. "A bargain
at the price!"

"Not here!" said the Christmas carolers.
"We can't hear ourselves sing!"

They moved back a few feet
and bumped right into Mitzi Blitzi.

"Why don't you kids watch
where you're going?" she snapped.

Weaver and Little Sunshine moved away again and found themselves right in front of the toy shop. The window was full of wonderful toys.

"Wouldn't it be great if Pa Christmas brought us that wind-up train set for our clubhouse?" said Weaver.

"If we don't have a tree he might not bring us anything," said Little Sunshine. "I sure hope we can sell some ornaments!"

Suddenly Big Bear, the town bully, swaggered up to them. "What's all that junk in the box?" he asked with a sneer.

"None of your business," said Little Sunshine.

Big Bear laughed. Then he grabbed the box of ornaments and ran off with it.

Before Weaver and Little Sunshine could catch him, Big Bear ran over to the kettle for the poor and dumped the ornaments into it.

HELP
THE POOR

Then with a nasty "Ha!" he ran away.

Little Sunshine and Weaver looked at the kettle and the sign next to it which read "HELP THE POOR."

Then they both thought for a moment.

"I'll bet that poor mouse family in Blackpitch Hollow would like to have our ornaments," said Little Sunshine.

"Yes," said Weaver. "They've got fourteen children."

"That's a lot of mouths to feed," said Little Sunshine. She took her gingerbread bear from her pocket and placed it inside the kettle.

Weaver put his in too.

"Maybe Pa Christmas will find our clubhouse even without a tree," sighed Little Sunshine.

"He just might," said Old Wolfgang, who had been watching. "On the other hand, a tree would make his job a lot easier."

Old Wolfgang led Weaver and Little Sunshine back to his lot.

"Please take this little tree," he said. "It's really too small to sell, and I don't want it to end up as firewood. Besides, it will help Pa Christmas to find you."

Weaver and Little Sunshine jumped for joy!

"I have one gingerbread bear left," said
Ollie Arwood. "I think it belongs on top
of your tree."

"Thank you! Thank you!" cried Weaver and Little Sunshine.

Then Ollie gave them a ride home on Crazy Horse's back.

All afternoon, while the wind whistled and the snow fell, Weaver Bear and Little Sunshine sat inside their clubhouse making ornaments.

They wanted their tree to be ready when Pa Christmas came to Puttyville.

Late that night Pa Christmas did find their clubhouse. And what he left under their little tree was sure to make them very happy!